★ THE ★
UNITED
STATES
PRESIDENTS

JAMES BUCHANAN

Megan M. Gunderson

Checkerboard
Library

An Imprint of Abdo Publishing
abdobooks.com

ABDOBOOKS.COM

Published by Abdo Publishing, a division of ABDO, PO Box 398166, Minneapolis, Minnesota 55439. Copyright © 2021 by Abdo Consulting Group, Inc. International copyrights reserved in all countries. No part of this book may be reproduced in any form without written permission from the publisher. Checkerboard Library™ is a trademark and logo of Abdo Publishing.

Printed in the United States of America, North Mankato, Minnesota
052020
092020

THIS BOOK CONTAINS
RECYCLED MATERIALS

Design: Emily O'Malley, Kelly Doudna, Mighty Media, Inc.
Production: Mighty Media, Inc.
Editor: Liz Salzmann

Cover Photograph: Getty Images
Interior Photographs: Albert de Bruijn/iStockphoto, p. 37; Andre Jenny/Alamy, p. 33; AP Images, p. 36; Getty Images, pp. 5, 23; Library of Congress, pp. 6 (James K. Polk), 7 (Harpers Ferry), 13, 14, 15, 16, 18, 19, 20, 24, 25, 28, 29, 40; The London Art Archive/Alamy, p. 31; Michael Snell/Alamy, p. 27; National Archives, p. 17; North Wind Picture Archives, pp. 6, 11; Pete Souza/Flickr, p. 44; Shutterstock Images, pp. 38, 39; Time Life Pictures/Getty Images, p. 32; Wikimedia Commons, pp. 7, 21, 30, 40 (George Washington), 42

Library of Congress Control Number: 2019956473

Publisher's Cataloging-in-Publication Data
Names: Gunderson, Megan M., author.
Title: James Buchanan / by Megan M. Gunderson
Description: Minneapolis, Minnesota : Abdo Publishing, 2021 | Series: The United States presidents | Includes online resources and index.
Identifiers: ISBN 9781532193408 (lib. bdg.) | ISBN 9781098212049 (ebook)
Subjects: LCSH: Buchanan, James, 1791-1868--Juvenile literature. | Presidents--Biography--Juvenile literature. | Presidents--United States--History--Juvenile literature. | Legislators--United States—Biography--Juvenile literature. | Politics and government--Biography--Juvenile literature.
Classification: DDC 973.68092--dc23

★ CONTENTS ★

James Buchanan

James Buchanan served as the fifteenth US president. When he took office in 1857, he was nearly 66 years old. Buchanan had already worked in politics for more than 40 years.

Buchanan had a respected political career. He was a member of the Pennsylvania House of Representatives. Buchanan also served in the US House of Representatives and the US Senate. He was minister to Russia and to Great Britain. Buchanan also served as **secretary of state**.

As president, Buchanan faced a difficult time in the nation's history. The Northern and Southern states were arguing over slavery. The country was about to split apart.

President Buchanan tried to keep the country united. However, the slavery problem proved too difficult to fix. Before his term ended, several Southern states left the Union.

Buchanan disagreed with this action. Yet he could find no way to stop it. Soon after Buchanan left the White House, the American **Civil War** began.

James Buchanan

★ TIMELINE ★

1791

On April 23, James Buchanan was born in Cove Gap, Pennsylvania.

1812

Buchanan became a lawyer.

1814

Buchanan's political career began in the Pennsylvania House of Representatives.

1834

Buchanan began serving in the US Senate.

1809

Buchanan graduated from Dickinson College in Carlisle, Pennsylvania.

1830s

Buchanan served as minister to Russia.

1845

Under President James K. Polk, Buchanan became secretary of state.

1821

Buchanan began serving in the US House of Representatives.

1853

President Franklin Pierce appointed Buchanan minister to Great Britain.

1857

Buchanan became the fifteenth US president. He supported the *Dred Scott* decision.

1861

Buchanan retired to Wheatland. The American Civil War began.

1868

On June 1, James Buchanan died.

1849

Buchanan retired as secretary of state and moved to Wheatland.

1854

Buchanan signed the Ostend Manifesto.

1859

John Brown led a rebellion at Harpers Ferry.

1866

Mr. Buchanan's Administration on the Eve of the Rebellion was published.

" We ought to do justice in a kindly spirit to all nations **and require justice from them in return."**

JAMES BUCHANAN

DID YOU KNOW?

★ James Buchanan's nickname was "Old Buck."

★ Buchanan is the only US president who was born in the state of Pennsylvania.

★ President Buchanan was his niece Harriet Lane's guardian. She accompanied him to Great Britain while he was minister there. Then, she served as White House hostess for her unmarried uncle. She became very popular in Washington, DC.

★ John C. Breckinridge took office at age 36. He is the youngest US vice president in American history.

Young James

James Buchanan was born in Cove Gap, Pennsylvania, on April 23, 1791. His parents were James and Elizabeth Speer Buchanan. James was the second of their 11 children.

James's father was an Irish **immigrant**. He was a successful storekeeper and landowner. He taught James important business skills. Elizabeth taught James to love books and his country.

James went to school in nearby Mercersburg, Pennsylvania. When he was 16, James entered Dickinson College in Carlisle, Pennsylvania. He graduated in 1809.

James then studied law in Lancaster, Pennsylvania. In 1812, he became a lawyer. James was smart and worked hard. He quickly became successful.

During this time, James briefly served in the **War of 1812**. He helped defend Baltimore, Maryland. Soon afterward, he began his career in politics.

FAST FACTS

BORN: April 23, 1791

WIFE: never married

CHILDREN: none

POLITICAL PARTY: Democrat

AGE AT INAUGURATION: 65

YEARS SERVED: 1857–1861

VICE PRESIDENT: John C. Breckinridge

DIED: June 1, 1868, age 77

Dickinson College is named for
Pennsylvania governor John Dickinson.

Politics and Tragedy

Buchanan's political career began in the Pennsylvania House of Representatives. At the time he was elected, Buchanan was a **Federalist**. He served from 1814 to 1816.

Buchanan became engaged to Ann Caroline Coleman in 1819. Rumors and arguments led to the end of their engagement. Soon after, Ann died. Buchanan never married. He remains the nation's only unmarried president.

In 1820, Buchanan was elected to the US House of Representatives. He served from 1821 to 1831. There, he was chairman of the House Committee on the **Judiciary**.

As chairman, Buchanan served as **prosecutor** in an 1831 **impeachment** trial. James H. Peck was on trial. Peck was a US district court judge in Missouri.

Missouri lawyer Luke Lawless had spoken out against Peck in a newspaper article. In it, he criticized several of Peck's court decisions.

Peck had sent Lawless to jail. He had also stopped Lawless from practicing law for 18 months. Buchanan argued that Peck had misused his powers as a judge. However, the US Senate found Peck innocent.

Ann Coleman's family was upset with Buchanan after her death. They did not let him attend her funeral.

Serving His Country

In the early 1830s, President Andrew Jackson made Buchanan minister to Russia. As minister, Buchanan arranged the first trade treaty between Russia and the United States.

Andrew Jackson was president from 1829 to 1837.

After returning from Russia, Buchanan was elected to the US Senate. He worked there from 1834 to 1845. Senator Buchanan served as chairman of the Committee on Foreign Relations. This group handles relations between the United States and other countries.

Senator Buchanan was also chairman of another committee. As part of this group, Buchanan defeated a proposed gag rule. The gag rule would have prevented people from introducing **petitions** against slavery in the Senate. Without the gag rule, the Senate was allowed to hear the petitions.

Buchanan gained valuable experience working in foreign countries. This helped prepare him for being secretary of state and president.

In 1845, Buchanan became President James K. Polk's **secretary of state**. At the time, the United States had problems to settle with other countries. As secretary, Buchanan helped settle a border disagreement with England over the Oregon Territory.

Buchanan also tried to settle a border argument with Mexico. But his attempts failed. The disagreement led to the **Mexican-American War**.

In 1846, Pennsylvania congressman David Wilmot proposed the Wilmot Proviso. It would have banned slavery in any territory gained from Mexico.

Buchanan morally opposed slavery. However, he believed slavery was legal according to the US **Constitution**. Buchanan

James K. Polk was president from 1845 to 1849.

believed in always following the law. So, he opposed Wilmot's ideas.

The country continued to argue about slavery. So, Kentucky senator Henry Clay proposed a group of new laws. These became the Compromise of 1850. Buchanan supported this.

Part of the Compromise of 1850 attempted to keep the same number of free and slave states in the Senate. Another part was the Fugitive Slave Law. This law stated rules for returning runaway slaves to their owners.

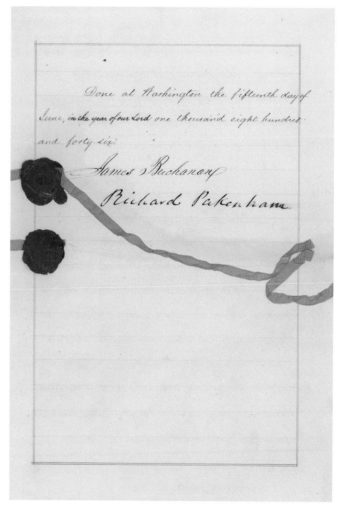

Done at Washington the fifteenth day of June, in the year of our Lord one thousand eight hundred and forty six.

James Buchanan

Richard Pakenham

In 1846, Buchanan signed the treaty that established Oregon's northern border.

A New Position

President Polk's term ended in 1849. At that time, Buchanan retired as **secretary of state**. He moved to a new house near Lancaster. It was called Wheatland.

There, Buchanan planned his campaign for the 1852 election. He had joined the **Democratic** Party when the **Federalist** Party broke up. Now, Buchanan hoped the Democrats would nominate him for president.

Franklin Pierce served one term as president, from 1853 to 1857.

Buchanan had a lot of political experience. So, many Democrats believed he would make a good candidate. Yet they nominated Franklin Pierce for president.

Buchanan supported Pierce during the campaign. Pierce won the 1852 election. In 1853, he made Buchanan minister to Great Britain.

While minister, Buchanan became involved in Pierce's efforts to gain Cuba. In 1854, Buchanan signed the

Signing the Ostend Manifesto earned Buchanan
support in the South. This helped him win
the presidential nomination in 1856.

Ostend Manifesto. It recommended that the United States
seize Cuba from Spain.

Many Americans disagreed with this plan. But others
believed gaining Cuba was a good idea. The United States
would get more land. And, many Southerners wanted
Cuba to become a slave state. In the end, the government
did not take over Cuba.

The Election of 1856

In 1856, the **Democrats** nominated Buchanan to run for president. His **running mate** was John C. Breckinridge of Kentucky. Former president Millard Fillmore ran as the **American** Party candidate. John C. Frémont ran for the new **Republican** Party.

The Republican Party had formed in 1854. It opposed the spread of slavery. Many people who were against slavery joined this new party. This included some Democrats.

Still, Buchanan won the election. He received fewer than half the **popular votes**. However, he won the most electoral votes. Buchanan won 174 electoral votes. Frémont received 114, and Fillmore received just eight.

John C. Breckinridge

John Wood photographed Buchanan's inauguration. This is the first known photograph of a presidential inauguration.

On March 4, 1857, Buchanan was **inaugurated** president. He became president as the slavery **debate** reached its peak. Still, Buchanan hoped the problem would be settled in court.

SUPREME COURT APPOINTMENT

NATHAN CLIFFORD: 1858

PRESIDENT BUCHANAN'S CABINET

ONE TERM
March 4, 1857–March 4, 1861

- ★ **STATE:** Lewis Cass
  Jeremiah S. Black (from December 17, 1860)
- ★ **TREASURY:** Howell Cobb
  Philip F. Thomas (from December 12, 1860)
  John A. Dix (from January 15, 1861)
- ★ **WAR:** John B. Floyd
- ★ **NAVY:** Isaac Toucey
- ★ **ATTORNEY GENERAL:** Jeremiah S. Black
  Edwin M. Stanton (from December 22, 1860)
- ★ **INTERIOR:** Jacob Thompson

Buchanan (*fourth from left*) and his cabinet

Dred Scott

Two days after Buchanan took office, the US **Supreme Court** decided the *Dred Scott* case. Most people hoped this important case would settle the slavery issue.

Dred Scott was a Missouri slave. He had once traveled with his owner to Illinois and the Wisconsin Territory. After returning to Missouri, Scott **sued** for his freedom. He had lived in a free state and a free territory. So, Scott argued he was a free man.

On March 6, 1857, the Supreme Court ruled against Scott. **Chief Justice** Roger B. Taney stated that slaves were property. He argued that a person could not be denied his property. And, he said that slaves had no right to sue in court.

Dred Scott

Two of John Brown's sons died in
the fighting at Harpers Ferry.

trouble leading a divided nation. Northerners were upset
that Buchanan defended slavery and the South. It was
certain the **Democrats** would not nominate Buchanan for a
second term.

Last Days in Office

During Buchanan's last four months in office, seven Southern states **seceded**. South Carolina, Mississippi, Florida, Alabama, Georgia, Louisiana, and Texas left the Union. They started their own country called the Confederate States of America.

Buchanan was against these actions. But he was torn. He felt there was no legal way to stop the states. However, he also felt they had no legal right to separate.

In January 1861, Buchanan sent supplies to Fort Sumter in South Carolina. This US fort was now in Confederate territory. Confederate forces surrounded the fort. They forced the supply ships to turn back. Before Buchanan could try to help the fort again, his term ended.

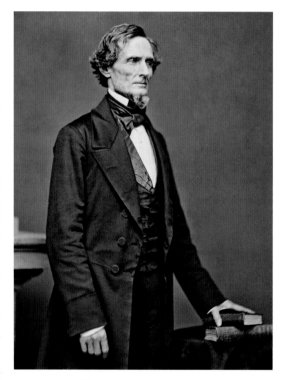

Jefferson Davis was the president of the Confederate States of America.

Confederate forces fired on Fort Sumter on April 12, 1861. This sparked the American Civil War.

After the White House

On March 4, 1861, Buchanan's long political career ended. That day, **Republican** Abraham Lincoln became the sixteenth US president.

Buchanan died at Wheatland and was buried in Lancaster, Pennsylvania.

Buchanan then retired to Wheatland. Soon after, the American **Civil War** began. During the war, Buchanan strongly supported the Union.

At the time, many people blamed Buchanan for not preventing the war. So, in 1866, he published *Mr. Buchanan's Administration on the Eve of the **Rebellion***. The work defended his actions during his time in office.

Wheatland is now a historic site
that people can visit.

James Buchanan died on June 1, 1868. Today, he is praised for delaying the war in the hope of peace. Many people believe he did what he could against impossible odds.

BRANCHES OF GOVERNMENT

The US government is divided into three branches. They are the executive, legislative, and judicial branches. This division is called a separation of powers. Each branch has some power over the others. This is called a system of checks and balances.

★ EXECUTIVE BRANCH

The executive branch enforces laws. It is made up of the president, the vice president, and the president's cabinet. The president represents the United States around the world. He or she oversees relations with other countries and signs treaties. The president signs bills into law and appoints officials and federal judges. He or she also leads the military and manages government workers.

★ LEGISLATIVE BRANCH

The legislative branch makes laws, maintains the military, and regulates trade. It also has the power to declare war. This branch consists of the Senate and the House of Representatives. Together, these two houses make up Congress. Each state has two senators. A state's population determines the number of representatives it has.

★ JUDICIAL BRANCH

The judicial branch interprets laws. It consists of district courts, courts of appeals, and the Supreme Court. District courts try cases. If a person disagrees with a trial's outcome, he or she may appeal. If a court of appeals supports the ruling, a person may appeal to the Supreme Court. The Supreme Court also makes sure that laws follow the US Constitution.

THE PRESIDENT ★

★ QUALIFICATIONS FOR OFFICE

To be president, a person must meet three requirements. A candidate must be at least 35 years old and a natural-born US citizen. He or she must also have lived in the United States for at least 14 years.

★ ELECTORAL COLLEGE

The US presidential election is an indirect election. Voters from each state choose electors to represent them in the Electoral College. The number of electors from each state is based on the state's population. Each elector has one electoral vote. Electors are pledged to cast their vote for the candidate who receives the highest number of popular votes in their state. A candidate must receive the majority of Electoral College votes to win.

★ TERM OF OFFICE

Each president may be elected to two four-year terms. Sometimes, a president may only be elected once. This happens if he or she served more than two years of the previous president's term.

The presidential election is held on the Tuesday after the first Monday in November. The president is sworn in on January 20 of the following year. At that time, he or she takes the oath of office:

> *I do solemnly swear (or affirm) that I will faithfully execute the office of President of the United States, and will to the best of my ability, preserve, protect and defend the Constitution of the United States.*

LINE OF SUCCESSION

The Presidential Succession Act of 1947 defines who becomes president if the president cannot serve. The vice president is first in the line of succession. Next are the Speaker of the House and the President Pro Tempore of the Senate. If none of these individuals is able to serve, the office falls to the president's cabinet members. They would take office in the order in which each department was created:

Secretary of State

Secretary of the Treasury

Secretary of Defense

Attorney General

Secretary of the Interior

Secretary of Agriculture

Secretary of Commerce

Secretary of Labor

Secretary of Health and Human Services

Secretary of Housing and Urban Development

Secretary of Transportation

Secretary of Energy

Secretary of Education

Secretary of Veterans Affairs

Secretary of Homeland Security

THEIR TERMS ★

LEFT OFFICE	TERMS SERVED	VICE PRESIDENT
March 4, 1797	Two	John Adams
March 4, 1801	One	Thomas Jefferson
March 4, 1809	Two	Aaron Burr, George Clinton
March 4, 1817	Two	George Clinton, Elbridge Gerry
March 4, 1825	Two	Daniel D. Tompkins
March 4, 1829	One	John C. Calhoun
March 4, 1837	Two	John C. Calhoun, Martin Van Buren
March 4, 1841	One	Richard M. Johnson
April 4, 1841	Died During First Term	John Tyler
March 4, 1845	Completed Harrison's Term	Office Vacant
March 4, 1849	One	George M. Dallas
July 9, 1850	Died During First Term	Millard Fillmore
March 4, 1853	Completed Taylor's Term	Office Vacant
March 4, 1857	One	William R.D. King
March 4, 1861	One	John C. Breckinridge
April 15, 1865	Served One Term, Died During Second Term	Hannibal Hamlin, Andrew Johnson
March 4, 1869	Completed Lincoln's Second Term	Office Vacant
March 4, 1877	Two	Schuyler Colfax, Henry Wilson
March 4, 1881	One	William A. Wheeler

Franklin D. Roosevelt

John F. Kennedy

Ronald Reagan

	PRESIDENT	PARTY	TOOK OFFICE
20	James A. Garfield	Republican	March 4, 1881
21	Chester Arthur	Republican	September 20, 1881
22	Grover Cleveland	Democrat	March 4, 1885
23	Benjamin Harrison	Republican	March 4, 1889
24	Grover Cleveland	Democrat	March 4, 1893
25	William McKinley	Republican	March 4, 1897
26	Theodore Roosevelt	Republican	September 14, 1901
27	William Taft	Republican	March 4, 1909
28	Woodrow Wilson	Democrat	March 4, 1913
29	Warren G. Harding	Republican	March 4, 1921
30	Calvin Coolidge	Republican	August 3, 1923
31	Herbert Hoover	Republican	March 4, 1929
32	Franklin D. Roosevelt	Democrat	March 4, 1933
33	Harry S. Truman	Democrat	April 12, 1945
34	Dwight D. Eisenhower	Republican	January 20, 1953
35	John F. Kennedy	Democrat	January 20, 1961

LEFT OFFICE	TERMS SERVED	VICE PRESIDENT
September 19, 1881	Died During First Term	Chester Arthur
March 4, 1885	Completed Garfield's Term	Office Vacant
March 4, 1889	One	Thomas A. Hendricks
March 4, 1893	One	Levi P. Morton
March 4, 1897	One	Adlai E. Stevenson
September 14, 1901	Served One Term, Died During Second Term	Garret A. Hobart, Theodore Roosevelt
March 4, 1909	Completed McKinley's Second Term, Served One Term	Office Vacant, Charles Fairbanks
March 4, 1913	One	James S. Sherman
March 4, 1921	Two	Thomas R. Marshall
August 2, 1923	Died During First Term	Calvin Coolidge
March 4, 1929	Completed Harding's Term, Served One Term	Office Vacant, Charles Dawes
March 4, 1933	One	Charles Curtis
April 12, 1945	Served Three Terms, Died During Fourth Term	John Nance Garner, Henry A. Wallace, Harry S. Truman
January 20, 1953	Completed Roosevelt's Fourth Term, Served One Term	Office Vacant, Alben Barkley
January 20, 1961	Two	Richard Nixon
November 22, 1963	Died During First Term	Lyndon B. Johnson

Barack Obama

	PRESIDENT	PARTY	TOOK OFFICE
36	Lyndon B. Johnson	Democrat	November 22, 1963
37	Richard Nixon	Republican	January 20, 1969
38	Gerald Ford	Republican	August 9, 1974
39	Jimmy Carter	Democrat	January 20, 1977
40	Ronald Reagan	Republican	January 20, 1981
41	George H.W. Bush	Republican	January 20, 1989
42	Bill Clinton	Democrat	January 20, 1993
43	George W. Bush	Republican	January 20, 2001
44	Barack Obama	Democrat	January 20, 2009
45	Donald Trump	Republican	January 20, 2017

★ PRESIDENTS MATH GAME ★

Have fun with this presidents math game! First, study the list above and memorize each president's name and number. Then, use math to figure out which president completes each equation below.

1. William Taft – James Buchanan = ?

2. James Buchanan + William McKinley = ?

3. Barack Obama – James Buchanan = ?

Answers: 1. Zachary Taylor (27 – 15 = 12)
2. Ronald Reagan (15 + 25 = 40)
3. Warren G. Harding (44 – 15 = 29)